Bob Ross® and Peapod the Squirrel

by Robb Pearlman

Illustrated by Bob Ross with Jason Kayser

RP|KIDS
PHILADELPHIA

Running Press Kids
Hachette Book Group
1290 Avenue of the Americas, New York, NY 10104
www.runningpress.com/rpkids
@RP_Kids

Printed in China

First Edition: October 2019

Published by Running Press Kids, an imprint of Perseus Books, LLC, a subsidiary of Hachette Book Group, Inc. The Running Press Kids name and logo is a trademark of the Hachette Book Group.

The Hachette Speakers Bureau provides a wide range of authors for speaking events. To find out more, go to www.hachettespeakersbureau.com or call (866) 376-6591.

The publisher is not responsible for websites (or their content) that are not owned by the publisher.

Text written by Robb Pearlman.
Cover and interior illustrations by Jason Kayser.
Print book cover and interior design by Jason Kayser.

Library of Congress Control Number: 2018959486

ISBNs: 978-0-7624-6779-2 (hardcover), 978-0-7624-6780-8 (ebook), 978-0-7624-6795-2 (ebook), 978-0-7624-6794-5 (ebook)

APS

10 9 8 7 6 5 4 3 2

My little squirrel friend,
Peapod, needs a new home.
(He keeps dropping pepperoni
in my hair!)

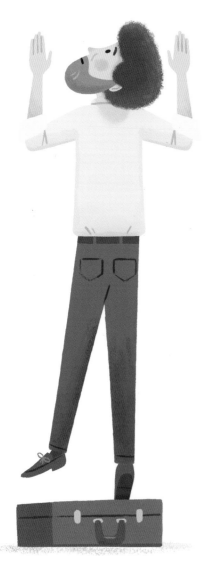

But we looked high . . .

and low, and we can't
find the right one.

Wait!

I have an idea!

Now, then. Let's have some fun!

We'll use blue to paint the sky.

And then we'll use white to
make happy little clouds that just float
around and have fun all day.

We can use a painting knife, too
(which is like a regular knife but you use it
to paint, not to make sandwiches).
We use the knife to spread a mix
of blue and brown and crimson to
make mountaintops.

Then we use a paintbrush
to make the mountain bottoms.
It's just that easy!

Peapod likes to ski, so let's add
some snow for him.

Oh no!
There's nowhere for Peapod to go!

Let's use green and blue to paint a meadow
before he gets to the bottom. Phew!

Peapod's quick stop made some
of the paint go splat. Oops!

Well, that was a happy accident!
Don't worry, Peapod.

We can do whatever we like in our world!

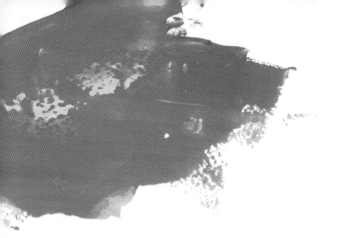

Let's use even more green
and blue and some brown and even some
yellow to paint a whole forest
of trees and bushes.

Here's your bravery test,
Peapod: add more blue . . . and
now there's a pond! Isn't that fantastic?
I knew you could do it!

How about a few more
trees and bushes and grassy things?

Let's just look at that
and enjoy it.

I think we're finished, don't you?

Now *this* is a home for my
little squirrel friend, Peapod.

And not a bad spot for me, too.

Happy Painting!

If you'd like to paint this picture yourself, here's what you'll need:

- One 18" x 24" canvas
- One 2-inch background brush
- One 1-inch landscape brush
- One liner brush
- One large painting knife
- One fan brush

Paint: Liquid White, Prussian Blue, Titanium White, Van Dyke Brown, Alizarin Crimson, Sap Green, Cadmium Yellow, Yellow Ochre, Bright Red, and Dark Sienna

But don't worry if your painting looks different at the end—that's what makes it great!